BEETHOVEN
SONATA NO. 17 IN D MINOR

OPUS 31, NO. 2
FOR THE PIANO

EDITED BY STEWART GORDON

AN ALFRED MASTERWORK EDITION

Cover art: Ludwig van Beethoven *(1770–1827)*
by Karl Stieler (1781–1858)
Oil on canvas, 1819
Beethoven-Haus, Bonn, Germany
Erich Lessing/Art Resource, NY
Additional art: © Planet Art

LUDWIG VAN BEETHOVEN

Sonata No. 17 in D Minor ("Tempest"), Op. 31, No. 2

Edited by Stewart Gordon

Foreword

About This Edition

Ludwig van Beethoven (1770–1827) is often regarded as a link between the balance and clarity of Classicism and the emotional intensity and freedom of Romanticism. In his 32 piano sonatas he experimented constantly with structure and content. These works span a period of almost 30 years of Beethoven's mature creative life. He used the sonatas as a workshop in which to try out innovations, many of his compositional techniques appearing in the sonatas first and then later in chamber or symphonic works.

The autograph manuscript for Sonata No. 17 in D Minor, Op. 31, No. 2, is lost; therefore, this edition is based on the two earliest editions, the first of which was published in Zürich, Switzerland, by Nägeli in April 1803, and the second published in Bonn, Germany, by Simrock later that year. Additionally, a number of other esteemed editions were referenced (see "Sources Consulted for This Edition" on page 3) when decisions have had to be made due to lack of clarity or inconsistency in the earliest editions, or when realization of ornamentation was open to question.

Recommended solutions to problems are suggested in footnotes in this edition. If, however, a problem is such that it is open to several solutions, other editors' conclusions are also often included. In this way students and their teachers are not only offered choices in individual cases but, more importantly, gain an awareness of the editorial and performance problems that attend studying and playing this music.

The insurmountable problems that arise in trying to distinguish between the staccato dot and the wedge in these works have led this editor to join ranks with most others in using but one marking (dot) for both symbols.

Like almost all other editors, I have chosen not to indicate pedaling markings in the sonatas except for those left by the composer. The matter of pedaling, especially as might be applicable to music of this era, must be based on innumerable choices that result from stylistic awareness and careful listening, these possibilities changing as different instruments or performance venues are encountered.

Both autographs and first editions contain inconsistencies. First editions especially are prone to many discrepancies, such as differences in articulation in parallel passages in expositions and recapitulations of movements in sonata-allegro form, or the many cases of an isolated note in passagework without the articulation shown for all its neighbors. Even those editors whose philosophy is to be as faithful to the composer as possible subscribe to the practice of correcting these small discrepancies without taking note of such through the addition of parentheses. This edition also subscribes to that practice to avoid cluttering the performer's pages with what would turn out to be a myriad of parenthetical changes. By the same token, this editor has proceeded with an attitude of caution and inquiry, so that such changes have been made only in the most obvious cases of error or omission. If, in the opinion of the editor, there seemed to be the slightest chance that such inconsistencies could represent conscious variation or musical intent on the part of the composer, the issue has been highlighted, either by the use of parentheses that show editorial additions or footnotes that outline discrepancies and discuss possible musical intent on the part of the composer.

Fingering in parentheses indicates alternative fingering. When a single fingering number attends a chord or two vertical notes, the number indicates the uppermost or lowermost note. Octaves on black keys are usually fingered 1-4, but it is acknowledged that such fingering may prove too much of a stretch for some hands. Thus, (4) in parenthesis indicates that players with small hands may want to substitute 1-5.

Ornaments such as trills, turns, and mordents are discussed in footnotes. When a single rapid appoggiatura or grace note is not footnoted, the performer should choose whether to execute it before the beat or on the beat. However, in some cases this editor indicates a preference for on-the-beat execution in the music by using a dotted line that connects the ornamental note with the base note with which it is to be played.

Sources Consulted for This Edition

Beethoven, Ludwig van. *Sonatas for Piano.* Edited by Eugen d'Albert. New York: Carl Fischer, 1981; originally published in 1902.

Beethoven, Ludwig van. *Sonaten für Klavier zu zwei Händen.* Edited by Claudio Arrau, revised by Lothar Hoffmann-Erbrecht. Frankfurt: C. F. Peters, 1973.

Beethoven, Ludwig van. *Sonatas for the Piano.* Edited by Hans von Bülow and Sigmund Lebert, translated by Theodore Baker. New York: G. Schirmer, 1894; currently distributed by Hal Leonard, Milwaukee.

Beethoven, Ludwig van. *Sonatas for Piano.* Edited by Alfredo Casella. Rome: G. Ricordi, 1919.

Beethoven, Ludwig van. *Complete Pianoforte Sonatas.* Edited by Harold Craxton, annotated Donald Francis Tovey. London: Associated Board of the Royal School of Music, 1931.

Beethoven, Ludwig van. *Sonaten für Klavier.* Edited by Peter Hauschild. Vienna and Mainz: Wiener Urtext Edition, Schott/Universal, 1999.

Beethoven, Ludwig van. *Sonaten für Klavier.* Edited by Louis Köhler and Adolf Ruthardt. Frankfurt: C. F. Peters; originally published in 1890.

Beethoven, Ludwig van. *Sonatas for Piano.* Edited by Carl Krebs. Los Angeles: Alfred Publishing; Kalmus Editions, originally published in 1898.

Beethoven, Ludwig van. *Sonaten für Klavier zu zwei Händen.* Edited by Carl Adolf Martienssen. New York: C. F. Peters, 1948.

Beethoven, Ludwig van. *Complete Piano Sonatas.* Edited by Heinrich Schenker with a new introduction by Carl Schachter. New York: Dover, 1975; originally published in 1934.

Beethoven, Ludwig van. *Sonatas for the Pianoforte.* Edited by Artur Schnabel. New York: Simon & Schuster, 1935.

Beethoven, Ludwig van. *Piano Sonatas.* Edited by Kendall Taylor. Melbourne: Allans Publishing PTY. Limited, 1989. Currently distributed by Elkin Music International, Inc. Pompano Beach, Florida.

Beethoven, Ludwig van. *Klaviersonaten.* Edited by B. A. Wallner, fingering by Conrad Hansen. Munich: G. Henle, 1952, 1980.

For Further Reading

The Letters of Beethoven; 3 vols. Edited and translated by Emily Anderson. London: St. Martin's Press, 1961.

Bach, Carl Philipp Emanuel. *Essay on the True Art of Playing Keyboard Instruments.* Translated and edited by William J. Mitchell. New York: W. W. Norton, 1949.

Czerny, Carl. *On the Proper Performance of All Beethoven's Works for the Piano.* Edited by Paul Badura-Skoda. Vienna: Universal Edition, 1970.

Dannreuther, Edward. *Musical Ornamentation.* 2 volumes. London: Novello & Co., 1893–95.

Hummel, Johann Nepomuk. *A Complete Theoretical and Practical Course of Instructions on the Art of Playing the Piano Forte, Commencing with the Simplest Elementary Principles and Including Every Information Requisite to the Most Finished Style of Performance.* London: T. Boosey & Co., 1829.

Kullak, Franz. *Beethoven's Piano Playing, with an Essay on the Execution of the Trill.* Translated by Theodore Baker. New York: G. Schirmer, 1901.

Newman, William S. *Beethoven on Beethoven: Playing His Piano Music His Way.* New York: W. W. Norton, 1988.

Newman, William S. *Performance Practices in Beethoven's Piano Sonatas.* New York: W. W. Norton, 1971.

Sonata No. 17 in D Minor

Ludwig van Beethoven (1770–1827)
Op. 31, No. 2

(a) Both Nägeli and Simrock show 𝄵. Bülow and Köhler erroneously show 𝄴. Pedal indications throughout the movement are in both first editions.

(b) Bülow, Casella, and Schnabel offer realizations for this turn:

Bülow and Casella: Schnabel:

ⓒ Bülow shows a disposition between the hands that is frequently recommended, that of continuing to play the triplet eighth notes
with the RH and crossing over with the LH to play the melody in the treble clef in measures 22–24 and 26–28, using the damper
pedal to sustain whole notes in the bass. This results in some degree of blurring in measures 23 and 27. Tovey and Casella permit
crossing in measures 30, 32, 34, 36, and 38–40, where use of the damper pedal does not blur the line, but compromises the staccato
marked on the *sf* quarter notes in measures 30, 32, 34, and 36. D'Albert, Schenker, and Schnabel recommend crossing only in
measures 38–40, where the *sf* quarter notes no longer carry a staccato mark (both in Nägeli and Simrock). This editor agrees with
crossing in measures 38–40, where the eighth-note triplet figure is high enough to make playing it with the LH awkward.

(d) The pedal markings in measures 147–152 and 157 through the downbeat of 163 are shown in both Nägeli and Simrock. Only d'Albert, Bülow, and Köhler change these markings. The remaining referenced editors follow the first editions, Casella and Schnabel pointing to the special pedal effect in footnotes. For those who find using full pedal objectionable, Taylor and Tovey suggest in their editions to hold the LH chord down and use discreet half-damping in the recitatives as a possibility. Charles Rosen also suggests this in his book on the sonatas. (*Beethoven's Piano Sonatas: A Short Companion*; Yale University Press; New Haven, 2002, footnote on page 170.) William S. Newman argues that the taste for color blurring was evidenced not only by Beethoven, but also by several composers of the period. (Newman: *Beethoven on Beethoven: Playing His Piano Music His Way*; W. W. Norton; New York; 1988; pp. 245–46.) Moreover, Newman traces anecdotal documentation through five parties that the composer stated he wanted the passage to sound like a voice in a vault.

(e) Both Nägeli and Simrock print the note D-flat as the final sixteenth note in measure 159. However, the note is changed to C in a copy from the collection of the *Gesellschaft der Musikfreunde* (Society of Friends of Music). This society was founded in Vienna in 1812 and holds one of the most important historic music collections in the world. An early acquisition came from the estate of Beethoven's lifelong friend the Archduke Rudolf (1788–1831). Thus, the change in measure 159 is reputed to have been made by Beethoven himself. Of the referenced editors, nine print the D-flat without comment and five print C or offer it as an alternative, Hauschild, Taylor, and Wallner providing notes.

(f) Both Nägeli and Simrock divide the arpeggios in measures 165–166 and 169–170 between two staves, almost identically.
The referenced editors are almost equally divided in the disposition of these arpeggios, six opting for execution of both by
the RH only, five suggesting a variety of ways to divide the arpeggios between the hands. In this editor's opinion, the arpeggio
in measures 165–166 can be executed comfortably with the RH. The one in measures 169–170 is more awkward, so the player
might want to consider the following division:

measures 169–170:

(g) The range limitation of Beethoven's keyboard forced him to write the RH of measures 193–196 differently from that of measures 59–62. Ten of the referenced editors present Beethoven's version without comment. Köhler offers an alternative version that is a transposition of measures 59–62. Casella refers to the possibility of such transposition in a footnote, but advises against it. This editor prefers to use the composer's version.

(a) Only Bülow offers advice with regard to this arpeggiation, suggesting it be slow with the uppermost note occurring on the downbeat.

(b) Schnabel and d'Albert recommend the following:

Bülow starts the run earlier; his notation suggests incorporating some degree of freedom:

Both Taylor and Tovey in written commentary suggest starting the run somewhere after the last quarter beat, but before the last eighth beat of the measure.

(c) Of the referenced editors, ten indicate by fingering that the trill begins on the main note. Arrau's fingering suggests starting on the upper auxiliary. Bülow provides a practical realization:  Apply also to measure 50.

(d) Disagreement is evidenced among the referenced editors as to how to execute the turn figure that appears in measures 10, 12, 14, 44, 46, 48, 52, 54, 56, 93, and 95. Arrau, Casella, Martienssen, Schenker, Schnabel, and Tovey recommend either of the following:

measure 10:   or:

d'Albert, Bülow, Köhler, and Taylor realize the figure as follows:

measure 10:   or:

Schnabel states that he does not like the first realization preferred by the second group as it "falsifies the rhythmic form." Taylor, on the other hand, argues that the realizations preferred by the first group "ignore Beethoven's important tie." Although seemingly a close call, this editor sides with the second group.

Interestingly, the two first editions show different placements of the turn sign, Nägeli placing it over the dotted sixteenth note in each case, and Simrock between the dotted sixteenth and the ensuing thirty-second note. (Nägeli's engraver slips once in measure 10, but otherwise the sign is represented as stated.)

Nägeli: Simrock:

ⓔ The turn symbol appears over the tied C on beat 2 in both Nägeli and Simrock. D'Albert, Arrau, Schnabel, and Taylor show realizations that begin after beat 2:

Schnabel and Taylor: d'Albert: Arrau:

Bülow, Casella, Köhler, Martienssen, Schenker, and Tovey opt for a version of the turn beginning before beat 2:

either: or:

Bülow acknowledges the first edition notation in a footnote, but deems its literal realization "doubtless not intended."
This editor joins the first group and prefers literal reading of the first edition.

ⓕ In both Nägeli and Simrock, measure 27 shows a slur in the RH between the first two chords. There is no slur in any of the subsequent figures in measures 28 and 29, nor in the repeat of the passage at measures 69, 70, and 71. Editors have addressed this inconsistency differently. Eight of the referenced editors simply apply the slur shown in measure 27 to all subsequent measures. Arrau, Krebs, Taylor, and Wallner apply the slur in measure 27 to measure 69, but leave the other measures (28, 29, 70, and 71) without slurs. Schenker places slurs in measures 27, 28, 69, and 70, but leaves the slurs off in measures 29 and 71. This editor has followed the pattern of the second group.

(g) Some performers may find interest in a tradition of rearranging the hands in measures 51, 53, and 55 so that they are not required to cross. Attributed to Adlof Henselt (1814–1889), this version was reproduced by Karl Klindworth (1830–1916) in his edition of the sonatas, and can be seen as an alternative in Casella's edition.

(h) Bülow suggests starting this run on beat 3 of the measure. D'Albert and Schnabel prefer to wait until immediately after the second half of beat 3.

(i) Of the editors whose indications are clear, nine start the trills in measures 100 and 101 on the main note. Arrau recommends the upper note, and Bülow uses the upper note in measure 100 (undoubtedly because of the immediately preceding D) and the main note in measure 101. Six indicate using after-notes (*nachschlag*) for each, and Schnabel prefers not using after-notes. This editor recommends the following:

measure 100:

(a) The low E that would allow the F in measure 42 to resolve downward was undoubtedly not available on Beethoven's piano. Bülow, Casella, Köhler, and Tovey indicate using it on today's piano. The other nine referenced editors and this one prefer following the first edition.

(b) In a historical context, this ornament when used by Beethoven is referred to as a *Pralltriller*. The composer typically applies it to the first note of a descending stepwise figure, notating it as a short mordent without a slash. Realizations of the figure should begin on the main note, on the beat, and its execution should be with a rhythmic cohesion that renders the figure more incisive than a melodic triplet does. This effect can be achieved by applying a strong accent to the first note:

measure 43: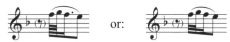

At tempo, a rapid triplet with an accented downbeat will probably be the only execution possible. However, editors have warned against the figure sounding like a melodic triplet rather than a snappy ornament. Schnabel uses the above notation. Bülow and Taylor try to capture its effect with the following:

     or:

This editor recommends the realization just described.

In this specific spot, however, Czerny writes out a realization that departs from the norm:

He gives his reason for such a departure as, "the bass note must come out smartly after the two small notes." (*Carl Czerny: On the Proper Performance of Beethoven's Works for the Piano*; edited with commentary by Paul Badura-Skoda; Universal Editions; Vienna, 1970, p. 44.) Incidentally, Czerny's realization is also easier to coordinate for many performers. Casella adopts Czerny's version. Tovey recommends the awkward combination of starting the ornament on the beat but accenting the third note of each figure.

ⓒ Both Nägeli and Simrock show the *p* mark on the downbeat of measure 73. However, measure 301, the analogous measure in the recapitulation, shows the *p* on beat 2 of the measure. This difference has led eleven of the referenced editors to deem measure 73 in error and change it to match measure 301. Only Wallner takes note of the change. Schenker and Taylor follow the first edition, with Taylor indicating in his notes to the movement that he believes the difference to be intentional.

ⓓ Nägeli shows a B-natural on the third sixteenth note of measure 93. All of the referenced editors use B-flat, as shown in Simrock; Hauschild notes the discrepancy.

(e) Although no *sf* appears in measure 175 in either Nägeli or Simrock, many editors add the sign on the downbeat in order to render the pattern here analogous to those that follow in measures 177–193. Thus, d'Albert, Bülow, Casella, Köhler, Martienssen, and Schenker add the marking without comment. Arrau, Krebs, and Taylor put it in parenthesis. Only Hauschild, Tovey, and Wallner follow the first edition, Tovey arguing against the addition in his notes.

(f) The LH fingering in measures 175–176 and 183–184 appears in Simrock, but not in Nägeli.

(g) Nägeli shows an erroneous E on beat 2 of measure 183 in the LH. Simrock corrected it.

27